Eugene Field's

Wynken, Blynken and Nod

Illustrated by

Ron Berg

Scholastic
New York • Toronto • London • Auckland • Sydney

ISBN 0-590-42422-X

Copyright © 1985 by Scholastic-TAB Publications Ltd., 123 Newkirk Road, Richmond Hill, Ontario, Canada L4C 3G5.
Illustrations copyright © 1985 by Ron Berg. Published by Scholastic Inc.

12 11 10 9 8 7 6 5 4 3 2 1   8 9/8 0 1 2 3/9

Wynken, Blynken and Nod one night
Sailed off in a wooden shoe,
Sailed on a river of crystal light
Into a sea of dew.

"Where are you going,

and what do you wish?"
The old Moon asked the three.

"We have come to fish
    for the herring fish
That live in this beautiful sea.
Nets of silver and gold have we,"
Said Wynken, Blynken
    and Nod.

The old Moon laughed
    and sang a song
As they rocked in the wooden shoe,
And the wind that sped them
    all night long
Ruffled the waves of dew.

The little stars were the herring fish
That lived in that beautiful sea.
"Now cast your nets
        wherever you wish,
But never afeared are we!"

So cried the stars
to the fishermen three,
Wynken, Blynken
and Nod.

All night long their nets they threw

For the fish in the twinkling foam,

Then down from the sky

    came the wooden shoe,

Bringing the fishermen home.

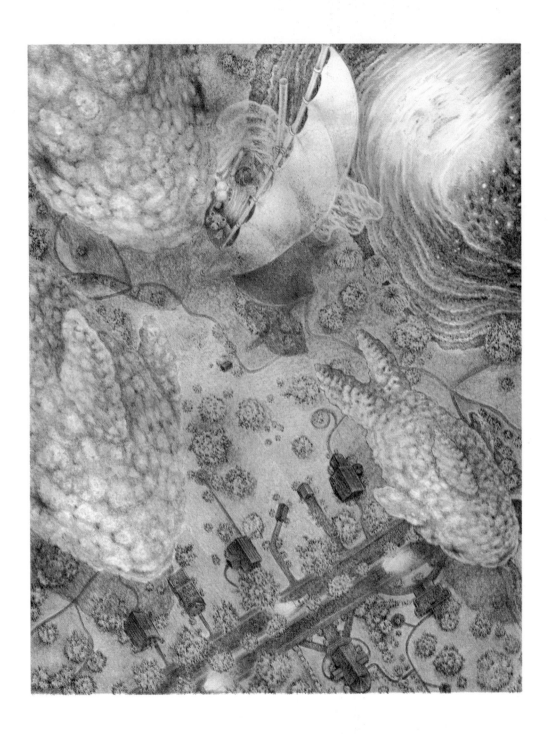

'Twas all so pretty a sail, it seemed
As if it could not be,
And some folk thought
    'twas a dream they'd dreamed
Of sailing that beautiful sea.

But I shall name you
    the fishermen three,
Wynken, Blynken
    and Nod.

Wynken and Blynken
    are two little eyes,
And Nod is a little head,
And the wooden shoe
    that sailed the skies
Is a wee one's trundle-bed.

So shut your eyes
    while Father sings
Of the wonderful sights that be,
And you shall see
    the beautiful things
As you rock in the misty sea

Where the old shoe rocked
the fishermen three,
Wynken, Blynken
and Nod.